Robert Browning

Lyrics of Life

Robert Browning

Lyrics of Life

ISBN/EAN: 9783744788113

Printed in Europe, USA, Canada, Australia, Japan

Cover: Foto ©Andreas Hilbeck / pixelio.de

More available books at **www.hansebooks.com**

BY

ROBERT BROWNING.

WITH ILLUSTRATIONS BY S. EYTINGE, JR.

BOSTON:
TICKNOR AND FIELDS.
1866.

CONTENTS.

LYRICS OF LIFE.

"HEAP CASSIA, SANDAL-BUDS, AND STRIPES."

HEAP cassia, sandal-buds, and stripes
 Of labdanum, and aloe-balls
Smeared with dull nard an Indian wipes
 From out her hair : (such balsam falls
 Down seaside mountain pedestals,
From summits where tired winds are fain,
Spent with the vast and howling main,
To treasure half their island-gain.)

And strew faint sweetness from some old
 Egyptian's fine worm-eaten shroud,
Which breaks to dust when once unrolled ;
 And shred dim perfume, like a cloud
 From chamber long to quiet vowed,
With mothed and dropping arras hung,
Mouldering the lute and books among
Of queen, long dead, who lived there young.

"OVER THE SEA OUR GALLEYS WENT."

OVER the sea our galleys went,
  With cleaving prows in order brave,
To a speeding wind and a bounding wave,—
  A gallant armament:
Each bark built out of a forest-tree,
  Left leafy and rough as first it grew,
And nailed all over the gaping sides,
Within and without, with black-bull hides,
Seethed in fat and suppled in flame,
To bear the playful billows' game;
So each good ship was rude to see,
Rude and bare to the outward view,
  But each upbore a stately tent;
Where cedar-pales in scented row
Kept out the flakes of the dancing brine:
And an awning drooped the mast below,
In fold on fold of the purple fine,
That neither noontide, nor star-shine,

Nor moonlight cold which maketh mad,
  Might pierce the regal tenement.
When the sun dawned, O, gay and glad
We set the sail and plied the oar ;
But when the night-wind blew like breath,
For joy of one day's voyage more,
We sang together on the wide sea,
Like men at peace on a peaceful shore ;
Each sail was loosed to the wind so free,
Each helm made sure by the twilight star,
And in a sleep as calm as death,
We, the strangers from afar,
  Lay stretched along, each weary crew
In a circle round its wondrous tent,
Whence gleamed soft light and curled rich scent,
  And with light and perfume, music too :
So the stars wheeled round, and the darkness past,
And at morn we started beside the mast,
And still each ship was sailing fast !

One morn the land appeared ! — a speck
Dim trembling betwixt sea and sky —
Avoid it, cried our pilot, check
  The shout, restrain the longing eye !
But the heaving sea was black behind
For many a night and many a day,
And land, though but a rock, drew nigh ;
So we broke the cedar-pales away,
Let the purple awning flap in the wind,
  And a statue bright was on every deck !
We shouted, every man of us,
And steered right into the harbor thus,
With pomp and pæan glorious.

An hundred shapes of lucid stone !
  All day we built a shrine for each —
A shrine of rock for every one —
Nor paused we till in the westering sun
  We sate together on the beach

To sing, because our task was done;
When lo! what shouts and merry songs!
What laughter all the distance stirs!
What raft comes loaded with its throngs
Of gentle islanders?
" The isles are just at hand," they cried;
" Like cloudlets faint at even sleeping,
Our temple-gates are opened wide,
Our olive-groves thick shade are keeping
For the lucid shapes you bring," — they cried.
O, then we awoke with sudden start
From our deep dream; we knew, too late,
How bare the rock, how desolate,
To which we had flung our precious freight:
Yet we called out — " Depart!
Our gifts, once given, must here abide:
Our work is done; we have no heart
To mar our work, though vain," — we cried.

.

"ALL SERVICE RANKS THE SAME WITH GOD.

ALL service ranks the same with God:
If now, as formerly He trod
Paradise, His presence fills
Our earth, each only as God wills
Can work, — God's puppets, best and worst,
Are we; there is no last nor first.

Say not " a small event"! Why "small"?
Costs it more pain than this, ye call
A "great event," should come to pass,
Than that? Untwine me from the mass
Of deeds which make up life, one deed
Power shall fall short in, or exceed!

"THE YEAR'S AT THE SPRING."

THE year 's at the spring,
　And day 's at the morn;
Morning 's at seven;
The hillside 's dew-pearled:
The lark 's on the wing;
The snail 's on the thorn;
God 's in his heaven —
All 's right with the world!

"A KING LIVED LONG AGO."

A KING lived long ago,
　In the morning of the world,
When earth was nigher heaven than now:
And the king's locks curled
Disparting o'er a forehead full
As the milk-white space 'twixt horn and horn
Of some sacrificial bull —
Only calm as a babe new-born:
For he was got to a sleepy mood,
So safe from all decrepitude,
From age with its bane so sure gone by,
(The Gods so loved him while he dreamed,)
That, having lived thus long, there seemed
No need the king should ever die.

Among the rocks his city was:
Before his palace, in the sun,
He sat to see his people pass,
And judge them every one
From its threshold of smooth stone.

2

They haled him many a valley-thief
Caught in the sheep-pens, — robber-chief,
Swarthy and shameless, — beggar cheat, —
Spy-prowler, — or rough pirate found
On the sea-sand left aground ;
And sometimes clung about his feet,
With bleeding lip and burning cheek,
A woman, bitterest wrong to speak
Of one with sullen thickset brows :
And sometimes from the prison-house
The angry priests a pale wretch brought,
Who through some chink had pushed and pressed,
On knees and elbows, belly and breast,
Worm-like into the temple, — caught
At last there by the very God,
Who ever in the darkness strode
Backward and forward, keeping watch
O'er his brazen bowls, such rogues to catch !
And these, all and every one,
The king judged, sitting in the sun.

His councillors, on left and right,
Looked anxious up, — but no surprise
Disturbed the king's old smiling eyes,
Where the very blue had turned to white.
'T is said, a Python scared one day
The breathless city, till he came,
With forky tongue and eyes on flame,
Where the old king sat to judge alway ;
But when he saw the sweepy hair,
Girt with a crown of berries rare
Which the God will hardly give to wear
To the maiden who singeth, dancing bare
In the altar-smoke by the pine-torch lights,
At his wondrous forest rites, —
Beholding this, he did not dare
Approach that threshold in the sun,
Assault the old king smiling there.
Such grace had kings when the world begun !

"YOU 'LL LOVE ME YET!"

YOU 'LL love me yet!—and I can tarry
   Your love's protracted growing:
June reared that bunch of flowers you carry
From seeds of April's sowing.

I plant a heartful now—some seed
At least is sure to strike
And yield—what you 'll not pluck indeed,
Not love, but, may be, like!

You 'll look at least on love's remains,
A grave's one violet:
Your look?—That pays a thousand pains.
What 's death?—You 'll love me yet!

"OVERHEAD THE TREE-TOPS MEET."

OVERHEAD the tree-tops meet—
   Flowers and grass spring 'neath one's feet—
There was naught above me, and naught below,
My childhood had not learned to know!
For, what are the voices of birds,
—Ay, and of beasts,—but words,—our words,
Only so much more sweet?
The knowledge of that with my life begun!
But I had so near made out the sun,
And counted your stars, the Seven and One,
Like the fingers of my hand:

Nay, I could all but understand
Wherefore through heaven the white moon ranges ;
And just when out of her soft fifty changes
No unfamiliar face might overlook me —
Suddenly God took me !

MARCHING ALONG.

KENTISH Sir Byng stood for his King,
    Bidding the crop-headed Parliament swing :
And, pressing a troop unable to stoop
And see the rogues flourish and honest folk droop,
Marched them along, fifty-score strong,
Great-hearted gentlemen, singing this song.

God for King Charles ! Pym and such carles
To the Devil that prompts 'em their treasonous parles !
Cavaliers, up ! Lips from the cup,
Hands from the pasty, nor bite take nor sup
Till you 're (*Chorus*) marching along, fifty-score strong,
Great-hearted gentlemen, singing this song.

Hampden to Hell, and his obsequies' knell
Serve Hazelrig, Fiennes, and young Harry as well !
England, good cheer ! Rupert is near !
Kentish and loyalists, keep we not here
            (*Cho.*) Marching along, fifty-score strong,
                Great-hearted gentlemen, singing this song ?

Then, God for King Charles ! Pym and his snarls
To the Devil that pricks on such pestilent carles !
Hold by the right, you double your might ;
So, onward to Nottingham, fresh for the fight,
            (*Cho.*) March we along, fifty-score strong,
                Great-hearted gentlemen, singing this song.

GIVE A ROUSE.

KING CHARLES, and who 'll do him right now?
  King Charles, and who 's ripe for fight now?
Give a rouse: here 's, in Hell's despite now,
King Charles!

Who gave me the goods that went since?
Who raised me the house that sank once?
Who helped me to gold I spent since?
Who found me in wine you drank once?
  (*Cho.*) King Charles, and who 'll do him right now?
      King Charles, and who 's ripe for fight now?
      Give a rouse: here 's, in Hell's despite now,
      King Charles!

To whom used my boy George quaff else,
By the old fool's side that begot him?
For whom did he cheer and laugh else,
While Noll's damned troopers shot him?
  (*Cho.*) King Charles, and who 'll do him right now?
      King Charles, and who 's ripe for fight now?
      Give a rouse: here 's, in Hell's despite now,
      King Charles!

BOOT AND SADDLE.

BOOT, saddle, to horse, and away!
  Rescue my Castle, before the hot day
Brightens to blue from its silvery gray,
        (*Cho.*) Boot, saddle, to horse, and away!

Ride past the suburbs, asleep as you'd say;
Many's the friend there will listen and pray
"God's luck to gallants that strike up the lay,
        (*Cho.*) Boot, saddle, to horse, and away!"

Forty miles off, like a roebuck at bay,
Flouts Castle Brancepeth the Roundheads' array:
Who laughs, "Good fellows ere this, by my fay,
        (*Cho.*) Boot, saddle, to horse, and away?"

Who? My wife Gertrude; that, honest and gay,
Laughs when you talk of surrendering, "Nay!
I've better counsellors; what counsel they?
        (*Cho.*) Boot, saddle, to horse, and away!"

"THERE 'S A WOMAN LIKE A DEW-DROP."

THERE 'S a woman like a dew-drop, she 's so purer than the
       purest ;
And her noble heart 's the noblest, yes, and her sure faith 's the
       surest :
And her eyes are dark and humid, like the depth on depth of lustre
Hid i' the harebell, while her tresses, sunnier than the wild-grape
       cluster,
Gush in golden-tinted plenty down her neck's rose-misted marble :
Then her voice's music . . . call it the well's bubbling, the bird's
       warble !

And this woman says, "My days were sunless and my nights
    were moonless,
Parched the pleasant April herbage, and the lark's heart's out-
    break tuneless,
If you loved me not!" And I who, — (ah, for words of flame!)
    adore her!
Who am mad to lay my spirit prostrate palpably before her, —
I may enter at her portal soon, as now her lattice takes me,
And by noontide as by midnight make her mine, as hers she
    makes me!

MY LAST DUCHESS.

THAT 'S my last Duchess painted on the wall,
    Looking as if she were alive; I call
That piece a wonder, now : Frà Pandolf's hands
Worked busily a day, and there she stands.
Will 't please you sit and look at her? I said
"Frà Pandolf" by design, for never read
Strangers like you that pictured countenance,
The depth and passion of its earnest glance,
But to myself they turned (since none puts by
The curtain I have drawn for you, but I)
And seemed as they would ask me, if they durst,
How such a glance came there; so, not the first
Are you to turn and ask thus. Sir, 't was not
Her husband's presence only, called that spot
Of joy into the Duchess' cheek : perhaps
Frà Pandolf chanced to say "Her mantle laps
Over my Lady's wrist too much," or "Paint
Must never hope to reproduce the faint
Half-flush that dies along her throat"; such stuff
Was courtesy, she thought, and cause enough
For calling up that spot of joy. She had

A heart . . . how shall I say ? . . . too soon made glad,
Too easily impressed ; she liked whate'er
She looked on, and her looks went everywhere.
Sir, 't was all one ! My favor at her breast,
The dropping of the daylight in the West,
The bough of cherries some officious fool
Broke in the orchard for her, the white mule
She rode with round the terrace, — all and each
Would draw from her alike the approving speech,
Or blush, at least. She thanked men, — good ; but thanked
Somehow . . . I know not how . . . as if she ranked
My gift of a nine hundred years old name
With anybody's gift. Who 'd stoop to blame
This sort of trifling ? Even had you skill
In speech — (which I have not) — to make your will
Quite clear to such an one, and say " Just this
Or that in you disgusts me ; here you miss,
Or there exceed the mark " — and if she let
Herself be lessoned so, nor plainly set
Her wits to yours, forsooth, and made excuse,
— E'en then would be some stooping, and I chuse
Never to stoop. O, Sir, she smiled, no doubt,
Whene'er I passed her ; but who passed without
Much the same smile ? This grew ; I gave commands ;
Then all smiles stopped together. There she stands
As if alive. Will 't please you rise ? We 'll meet
The company below, then. I repeat,
The Count your Master's known munificence
Is ample warrant that no just pretence
Of mine for dowry will be disallowed ;
Though his fair daughter's self, as I avowed
At starting, is my object. Nay, we 'll go
Together down, Sir ! Notice Neptune, though,
Taming a sea-horse, thought a rarity,
Which Claus of Innsbruck cast in bronze for me.

SOLILOQUY OF THE SPANISH CLOISTER.

G R-R-R — there go, my heart's abhorrence!
     Water your damned flower-pots, do!
If hate killed men, Brother Lawrence,
     God's blood, would not mine kill you!
What? your myrtle-bush wants trimming?
     O, that rose has prior claims, —
Needs its leaden vase filled brimming?
     Hell dry you up with its flames!

At the meal we sit together:
     Salve tibi! I must hear
Wise talk of the kind of weather,
     Sort of season, time of year:
Not a plenteous cork-crop: scarcely
     Dare we hope oak-galls, I doubt:
What 's the Latin name for " parsley "?
     What 's the Greek name for Swine's Snout?

Whew! We 'll have our platter burnished,
     Laid with care on our own shelf!
With a fire-new spoon we 're furnished,
     And a goblet for ourself,
Rinsed like something sacrificial
     Ere 't is fit to touch our chaps, —
Marked with L. for our initial!
     (He, he! There his lily snaps!)

Saint, forsooth! While brown Dolores
     Squats outside the Convent bank,
With Sanchicha, telling stories,
     Steeping tresses in the tank,
Blue-black, lustrous, thick like horse-hairs,
     — Can't I see his dead eye glow

Bright, as 't were a Barbary corsair's?
  (That is, if he 'd let it show!)

When he finishes refection,
  Knife and fork he never lays
Cross-wise, to my recollection,
  As do I, in Jesu's praise.
I, the Trinity illustrate,
  Drinking watered orange-pulp, —
In three sips the Arian frustrate;
  While he drains his at one gulp!

O, those melons! If he 's able
  We 're to have a feast; so nice!
One goes to the Abbot's table,
  All of us get each a slice.
How go on your flowers? None double?
  Not one fruit-sort can you spy?
Strange! — And I, too, at such trouble,
  Keep 'em close-nipped on the sly!

There 's a great text in Galatians,
  Once you trip on it, entails
Twenty-nine distinct damnations,
  One sure, if another fails.
If I trip him just a-dying,
  Sure of Heaven as sure can be,
Spin him round and send him flying
  Off to Hell, a Manichee!

Or, my scrofulous French novel,
  On gray paper with blunt type!
Simply glance at it, you grovel
  Hand and foot in Belial's gripe:
If I double down its pages
  At the woful sixteenth point,
When he gathers his greengages,
  Ope a sieve and slip it in 't!

Or, there 's Satan! — one might venture
  Pledge one's soul to him, yet leave
Such a flaw in the indenture
  As he 'd miss till, past retrieve,
Blasted lay that rose-acacia
  We 're so proud of! *Hy, Zy, Hine* . .
'St, there 's Vespers! *Plena gratiâ*
  Ave Virgo! Gr-r-r — you swine!

THROUGH THE METIDJA TO ABD-EL-KADR.

A S I ride, as I ride,
    With a full heart for my guide,
So its tide rocks my side,
As I ride, as I ride,
That, as I were double-eyed,
He, in whom our Tribes confide,
Is descried, ways untried
As I ride, as I ride.

As I ride, as I ride
To our Chief and his Allied,
Who dares chide my heart's pride
As I ride, as I ride?
Or are witnesses denied, —
Through the desert waste and wide
Do I glide unespied
As I ride, as I ride?

As I ride, as I ride,
When an inner voice has cried,
The sands slide, nor abide
(As I ride, as I ride)

O'er each visioned Homicide
That came vaunting (has he lied?)
To reside — where he died,
As I ride, as I ride.

As I ride, as I ride,
Ne'er has spur my swift horse plied,
Yet his hide, streaked and pied,
As I ride, as I ride,
Shows where sweat has sprung and dried,
— Zebra-footed, ostrich-thighed, —
How has vied stride with stride
As I ride, as I ride!

As I ride, as I ride,
Could I loose what Fate has tied,
Ere I pried, she should hide
As I ride, as I ride,
All that's meant me : satisfied
When the Prophet and the Bride
Stop veins I'd have subside
As I ride, as I ride!

COUNT GISMOND.

CHRIST God, who savest men, save most
    Of men Count Gismond who saved me!
Count Gauthier, when he chose his post,
  Chose time and place and company
To suit it; when he struck at length
My honor 't was with all his strength.

And doubtlessly ere he could draw
  All points to one, he must have schemed.

That miserable morning saw
   Few half so happy as I seemed,
While being dressed in Queen's array
   To give our Tourney prize away.

I thought they loved me, did me grace
   To please themselves; 't was all their deed :
God makes, or fair or foul, our face ;
   If showing mine so caused to bleed
My cousins' hearts, they should have dropped
A word, and straight the play had stopped.

They, too, so beauteous ! Each a queen
   By virtue of her brow and breast ;
Not needing to be crowned, I mean,
   As I do. E'en when I was dressed,
Had either of them spoke, instead
Of glancing sideways with still head !

But no : they let me laugh, and sing
   My birthday song quite through, adjust
The last rose in my garland, fling
   A last look on the mirror, trust
My arms to each an arm of theirs,
And so descend the castle-stairs, —

And come out on the morning troop
   Of merry friends who kissed my cheek,
And called me Queen, and made me stoop
   Under the canopy, — (a streak
That pierced it, of the outside sun,
Powdered with gold its gloom's soft dun,) —

And they could let me take my state
   And foolish throne amid applause
Of all come there to celebrate
   My Queen's day, — O, I think the cause
Of much was, they forgot no crowd
Makes up for parents in their shroud !

Howe'er that be, all eyes were bent
　Upon me, when my cousins cast
Theirs down; 't was time I should present
　The victor's crown, but . . . there, 't will last
No long time . . . the old mist again
Blinds me as then it did. How vain!

See! Gismond 's at the gate, in talk
　With his two boys: I can proceed.
Well, at that moment, who should stalk
　Forth boldly (to my face, indeed)
But Gauthier, and he thundered "Stay!"
And all stayed. "Bring no crowns, I say!"

"Bring torches! Wind the penance-sheet
　About her! Let her shun the chaste,
Or lay herself before their feet!
　Shall she, whose body I embraced
A night long, queen it in the day?
For Honor's sake no crowns, I say!"

I? What I answered? As I live
　I never fancied such a thing
As answer possible to give.
　What says the body when they spring
Some monstrous torture-engine's whole
Strength on it? No more says the soul.

Till out strode Gismond; then I knew
　That I was saved. I never met
His face before, but, at first view,
　I felt quite sure that God had set
Himself to Satan; who would spend
A minute's mistrust on the end?

He strode to Gauthier, in his throat
　Gave him the lie, then struck his mouth
With one back-handed blow that wrote
　In blood men's verdict there. North, South,

East, West, I looked.   The lie was dead,
And damned, and truth stood up instead.

This glads me most, that I enjoyed
    The heart of the joy, with my content
In watching Gismond unalloyed
    By any doubt of the event:
God took that on him, — I was bid
Watch Gismond for my part: I did.

Did I not watch him while he let
    His armorer just brace his greaves,
Rivet his hauberk, on the fret
    The while!   His foot . . . my memory leaves
No least stamp out, nor how anon
He pulled his ringing gauntlets on.

And e'en before the trumpet's sound
    Was finished, prone lay the false Knight,
Prone as his lie upon the ground:
    Gismond flew at him, used no sleight
Of the sword, but open-breasted drove,
Cleaving till out the truth he clove.

Which done, he dragged him to my feet
    And said, "Here die, but end thy breath
In full confession, lest thou fleet
    From my first, to God's second death!
Say hast thou lied?"   And "I have lied
To God and her," he said, and died.

Then Gismond, kneeling to me, asked
    — What safe my heart holds, though no word
Could I repeat now, if I tasked
    My powers forever, to a third
Dear even as you are.   Pass the rest
Until I sank upon his breast.

Over my head his arm he flung
    Against the world; and scarce I felt

His sword, that dripped by me and swung,
　　A little shifted in its belt, —
For he began to say the while
How South our home lay many a mile.

So 'mid the shouting multitude
　　We two walked forth to never more
Return.　My cousins have pursued
　　Their life, untroubled as before

3

I vexed them.   Gauthier's dwelling-place
God lighten !   May his soul find grace !

Our elder boy has got the clear
   Great brow ; tho' when his brother's black
Full eye shows scorn, it . . . Gismond here ?
   And have you brought my tercel back ?
I just was telling Adela
How many birds it struck since May.

THE LOST LEADER.

JUST for a handful of silver he left us,
   Just for a ribbon to stick in his coat, —
Found the one gift of which fortune bereft us,
   Lost all the others she lets us devote ;
They, with the gold to give, doled him out silver,
   So much was their's who so little allowed :
How all our copper had gone for his service !
   Rags, — were they purple, his heart had been proud !
We that had loved him so, followed him, honored him,
   Lived in his mild and magnificent eye,
Learned his great language, caught his clear accents,
   Made him our pattern to live and to die !
Shakespeare was of us, Milton was for us,
   Burns, Shelley, were with us, — they watch from their graves !
He alone breaks from the van and the freemen,
   He alone sinks to the rear and the slaves !

We shall march prospering, — not through his presence ;
   Songs may inspirit us, — not from his lyre ;
Deeds will be done, — while he boasts his quiescence,
   Still bidding crouch whom the rest bade aspire :

Blot out his name, then, — record one lost soul more,
　One task more declined, one more footpath untrod,
One more triumph for devils, and sorrow for angels,
　One wrong more to man, one more insult to God !
Life's night begins : let him never come back to us !
　There would be doubt, hesitation, and pain,
Forced praise on our part, the glimmer of twilight,
　Never glad confident morning again !
Best fight on well, for we taught him, — strike gallantly,
　Aim at our heart ere we pierce through his own ;
Then let him receive the new knowledge and wait us,
　Pardoned in Heaven, the first by the throne !

THE LOST MISTRESS.

ALL 'S over, then, — does truth sound bitter
　　As one at first believes ?
Hark, 't is the sparrows' good-night twitter
　About your cottage eaves !

And the leaf-buds on the vine are woolly,
　I noticed that, to-day ;
One day more bursts them open fully,
　— You know the red turns gray.

To-morrow we meet the same then, dearest ?
　May I take your hand in mine ?
Mere friends are we, — well, friends the merest
　Keep much that I 'll resign :

For each glance of that eye so bright and black, .
　Though I keep with heart's endeavor, —
Your voice, when you wish the snowdrops back,
　Though it stays in my soul forever ! —

— Yet I will but say what mere friends say,
  Or only a thought stronger;
I will hold your hand but as long as all may,
  Or so very little longer!

HOME THOUGHTS, FROM ABROAD.

OH, to be in England
  Now that April's there,
And whoever wakes in England
Sees, some morning, unaware,
That the lowest boughs and the brushwood sheaf
Round the elm-tree bole are in tiny leaf,
While the chaffinch sings on the orchard bough
In England — now!

And after April, when May follows,
And the white-throat builds, and all the swallows, —
Hark! where my blossomed pear-tree in the hedge
Leans to the field and scatters on the clover
Blossoms and dewdrops, — at the bent spray's edge, —
That's the wise thrush; he sings each song twice over,
Lest you should think he never could recapture
The first fine, careless rapture!
And though the fields look rough with hoary dew,
All will be gay when noontide wakes anew
The buttercups, the little children's dower,
— Far brighter than this gaudy melon-flower!

HOME THOUGHTS, FROM THE SEA.

NOBLY, nobly Cape Saint Vincent to the northwest died
    away ;
Sunset ran, one glorious blood-red, reeking into Cadiz Bay ;
Bluish mid the burning water, full in face Trafalgar lay ;
In the dimmest northeast distance, dawned Gibraltar grand and
    gray ;
" Here and here did England help me, — how can I help Eng-
    land ? " — say,
Whoso turns as I, this evening, turn to God to praise and pray,
While Jove's planet rises yonder, silent over Africa.

THE FLOWER'S NAME.

HERE 'S the garden she walked across,
    Arm in my arm, such a short while since :
Hark, now I push its wicket, the moss
    Hinders the hinges and makes them wince !
She must have reached this shrub ere she turned,
    As back with that murmur the wicket swung ;
For she laid the poor snail, my chance foot spurned,
    To feed and forget it the leaves among.

Down this side of the gravel-walk
    She went while her robe's edge brushed the box :
And here she paused in her gracious talk
    To point me a moth on the milk-white flox.
Roses, ranged in valiant row,
    I will never think that she passed you by !
She loves you noble roses, I know ;
    But yonder see, where the rock-plants lie !

This flower she stopped at, finger on lip,
    Stooped over, in doubt, as settling its claim;
Till she gave me, with pride to make no slip,
    Its soft meandering Spanish name.
What a name!   Was it love, or praise?
    Speech half-asleep, or song half-awake?
I must learn Spanish, one of these days,
    Only for that slow, sweet name's sake.

Roses, if I live and do well,
    I may bring her, one of these days,
To fix you fast with as fine a spell,
    Fit you each with his Spanish phrase!
But do not detain me now; for she lingers
    There, like sunshine over the ground,
And ever I see her soft white fingers
    Searching after the bud she found.

Flower, you Spaniard, look that you grow not,
    Stay as you are and be loved forever!
Bud, if I kiss you 't is that you blow not,
    Mind, the shut pink mouth opens never!
For while thus it pouts, her fingers wrestle,
    Twinkling the audacious leaves between,
Till round they turn and down they nestle, —
    Is not the dear mark still to be seen?

Where I find her not, beauties vanish;
    Whither I follow her, beauties flee;
Is there no method to tell her in Spanish
    June's twice June since she breathed it with me?
Come, bud, show me the least of her traces,
    Treasure my lady's lightest footfall
— Ah, you may flout and turn up your faces, —
    Roses, you are not so fair after all!

THE PIED PIPER OF HAMELIN.

HAMELIN Town 's in Brunswick,
　　By famous Hanover city ;
The river Weser, deep and wide,
Washes its wall on the southern side ;
A pleasanter spot you never spied ;
But, when begins my ditty,
　　Almost five hundred years ago,
　　To see the townsfolk suffer so
　　　From vermin, was a pity.

　　Rats !
They fought the dogs, and killed the cats,
　　And bit the babies in the cradles,
And ate the cheeses out of the vats,
　　And licked the soup from the cook's own ladles,
Split open the kegs of salted sprats,
Made nests inside men's Sunday hats,
And even spoiled the women's chats,
　　　By drowning their speaking
　　　With shrieking and squeaking
In fifty different sharps and flats.

At last the people in a body
　　To the Town Hall came flocking :
"'T is clear," cried they, " our Mayor 's a noddy ;
　　And as for our Corporation, — shocking
To think we buy gowns lined with ermine
For dolts that can't or won't determine
What 's best to rid us of our vermin !
You hope, because you 're old and obese,
To find in the furry civic robe ease ?
Rouse up, Sirs ! Give your brains a racking
To find the remedy we 're lacking,
Or, sure as fate, we 'll send you packing ! "

At this the Mayor and Corporation
Quaked with a mighty consternation.

An hour they sat in counsel,
   At length the Mayor broke silence :
" For a guilder I 'd my ermine gown sell ;
   I wish I were a mile hence !
It 's easy to bid one rack one's brain, —
I 'm sure my poor head aches again
I 've scratched it so, and all in vain.
O for a trap, a trap, a trap ! "
Just as he said this, what should hap
At the chamber door but a gentle tap ?
" Bless us," cried the Mayor, " what 's that ? "
(With the Corporation as he sat,
Looking little, though wondrous fat ;
Nor brighter was his eye, nor moister
Than a too long-opened oyster,
Save when at noon his paunch grew mutinous
For a plate of turtle green and glutinous)
" Only a scraping of shoes on the mat ?
Anything like the sound of a rat
Makes my heart go pit-a-pat ! "

" Come in ! " — the Mayor cried, looking bigger :
And in did come the strangest figure !
His queer long coat from heel to head
Was half of yellow and half of red ;
And he himself was tall and thin,
With sharp blue eyes, each like a pin,
And light loose hair, yet swarthy skin,
No tuft on cheek nor beard on chin,
But lips where smiles went out and in, —
There was no guessing his kith and kin !
And nobody could enough admire
The tall man and his quaint attire :
Quoth one : " It 's as my great-grandsire,
Starting up at the Trump of Doom's tone,
Had walked this way from his painted tomb-stone ! "

He advanced to the council-table :
And, " Please your honors," said he, " I 'm able,
By means of a secret charm, to draw
All creatures living beneath the sun,
That creep, or swim, or fly, or run,
After me so as you never saw !
And I chiefly use my charm
On creatures that do people harm,
The mole, and toad, and newt, and viper ;
And people call me the Pied Piper."
(And here they noticed round his neck
A scarf of red and yellow stripe,
To match with his coat of the selfsame check ;
And at the scarf's end hung a pipe ;
And his fingers, they noticed, were ever straying
As if impatient to be playing
Upon this pipe, as low it dangled
Over his vesture so old-fangled.)
" Yet," said he, " poor piper as I am,
In Tartary I freed the Cham
Last June from his huge swarms of gnats ;
I eased in Asia the Nizam
Of a monstrous brood of vampyre-bats :
And, as for what your brain bewilders,
If I can rid your town of rats
Will you give me a thousand guilders ? "
" One ? fifty thousand ! " — was the exclamation
Of the astonished Mayor and Corporation.

Into the street the Piper stept,
    Smiling first a little smile,
As if he new what magic slept
    In his quiet pipe the while ;
Then, like a musical adept,
To blow the pipe his lips he wrinkled,
And green and blue his sharp eyes twinkled
Like a candle flame where salt is sprinkled ;
And ere three shrill notes the pipe uttered,
You heard as if an army muttered ;

And the muttering grew to a grumbling ;
And the grumbling grew to a mighty rumbling,
And out of the houses the rats came tumbling.
Great rats, small rats, lean rats, brawny rats,
Brown rats, black rats, gray rats, tawny rats,
Grave old plodders, gay young friskers,
    Fathers, mothers, uncles, cousins,

Cocking tails and pricking whiskers,
    Families by tens and dozens,
Brothers, sisters, husbands, wives —
Followed the Piper for their lives.
From street to street he piped advancing,
And step for step they followed dancing,
Until they came to the river Weser
Wherein all plunged and perished,
— Save one who, stout as Julius Cæsar,
Swam across and lived to carry
(As he the manuscript he cherished)
To Rat-land home his commentary,
Which was, " At the first shrill notes of the pipe,
I heard a sound as of scraping tripe,
And putting apples, wondrous ripe,
Into a cider-press's gripe:
And a moving away of pickle-tub-boards,
And a leaving ajar of conserve-cupboards,
And a drawing the corks of train-oil-flasks,
And a breaking the hoops of butter-casks;
And it seemed as if a voice
(Sweeter far than by harp or by psaltery
Is breathed) called out, O rats, rejoice!
The world is grown to one vast drysaltery!
So munch on, crunch on, take your nuncheon,
Breakfast, supper, dinner, luncheon!
And just as a bulky sugar-puncheon,
All ready staved, like a great sun shone
Glorious scarce an inch before me,
Just as methought it said, Come, bore me!
— I found the Weser rolling o'er me."

You should have heard the Hamelin people
Ringing the bells till they rocked the steeple;
" Go," cried the Mayor, " and get long poles!
Poke out the nests and block up the holes!
Consult with carpenters and builders,
And leave in our town not even a trace
Of the rats!" — when suddenly up the face

Of the Piper perked in the market-place,
With a, "First if you please, my thousand guilders!"

A thousand guilders! The Mayor looked blue;
So did the Corporation too.
For council dinners made rare havock
With Claret, Moselle, Vin-de-Grave, Hock;
And half the money would replenish
Their cellar's biggest butt with Rhenish.
To pay this sum to a wandering fellow
With a gypsy coat of red and yellow!
"Beside," quoth the Mayor with a knowing wink,
"Our business was done at the river's brink;
We saw with our eyes the vermin sink,
And what's dead can't come to life I think.
So, friend, we're not the folks to shrink
From the duty of giving you something for drink,
And a matter of money to put in your poke;
But, as for the guilders, what we spoke
Of them, as you very well know, was in joke.
Beside, our losses have made us thrifty;
A thousand guilders! Come, take fifty!"

The Piper's face fell, and he cried,
"No trifling! I can't wait, beside!
I've promised to visit by dinner time
Bagdat, and accept the prime
Of the Head Cook's pottage, all he's rich in,
For having left, in the Caliph's kitchen,
Of a nest of scorpions no survivor, —
With him I proved no bargain-driver,
With you, don't think I'll bate a stiver!
And folks who put me in a passion
May find me pipe to another fashion."

"How?" cried the Mayor, "d'ye think I'll brook
Being worse treated than a Cook?
Insulted by a lazy ribald
With idle pipe and vesture piebald?

You threaten us, fellow?   Do your worst,
Blow your pipe there till you burst!"

Once more he stept into the street;
    And to his lips again
Laid his long pipe of smooth straight cane;
    And ere he blew three notes (such sweet
Soft notes as yet musician's cunning
    Never gave the enraptured air)
There was a rustling, that seemed like a bustling
Of merry crowds justling at pitching and hustling,
Small feet were pattering, wooden shoes clattering,
Little hands clapping, and little tongues chattering,
And, like fowls in a farm-yard when barley is scattering,
Out came the children running.
All the little boys and girls,
With rosy cheeks and flaxen curls,
And sparkling eyes and teeth like pearls,
Tripping and skipping, ran merrily after
The wonderful music with shouting and laughter.

The Mayor was dumb, and the Council stood
As if they were changed into blocks of wood,
Unable to move a step, or cry
To the children merrily skipping by, —
And could only follow with the eye
That joyous crowd at the Piper's back.
But how the Mayor was on the rack,
And the wretched Council's bosoms beat,
As the Piper turned from the High Street
To where the Weser rolled its waters
Right in the way of their sons and daughters!
However he turned from South to West,
And to Koppelberg Hill his steps addressed,
And after him the children pressed;
Great was the joy in every breast.
"He never can cross that mighty top!
He's forced to let the piping drop,
And we shall see our children stop!"

When, lo ! as they reached the mountain's side,
A wondrous portal opened wide,
As if a cavern was suddenly hollowed ;
And the Piper advanced and the children followed,
And when all were in to the very last,
The door in the mountain side shut fast.
Did I say all ? No. One was lame,
And could not dance the whole of the way ;
And in after years, if you would blame
His sadness, he was used to say, —
" It 's dull in our town since my playmates left !
I can't forget that I 'm bereft
Of all the pleasant sights they see,
Which the Piper also promised me ;
For he led us, he said, to a joyous land,
Joining the town and just at hand,
Where waters gushed and fruit-trees grew,
And flowers put forth a fairer hue,
And everything was strange and new ;
The sparrows were brighter than peacocks here,
And their dogs outran our fallow deer,
And honey-bees had lost their stings,
And horses were born with eagles' wings ;
And just as I became assured
My lame foot would be speedily cured,
The music stopped and I stood still,
And found myself outside the Hill,
Left alone against my will,
To go now limping as before,
And never hear of that country more ! "

Alas ! alas for Hamelin !
   There came into many a burgher's pate
   A text which says, that Heaven's Gate
   Opes to the Rich at as easy rate
As the needle's eye takes a camel in !
The Mayor sent East, West, North, and South
To offer the Piper by word of mouth,
   Wherever it was men's lot to find him,
Silver and gold to his heart's content,

If he 'd only return the way he went,
   And bring the children behind him.
But when they saw 't was a lost endeavor,
And Piper and dancers were gone forever,
They made a decree that lawyers never
   Should think their records dated duly
If, after the day of the month and year,
These words did not as well appear,
" And so long after what happened here
   On the Twenty-second of July,
Thirteen hundred and Seventy-six " :
And the better in memory to fix
The place of the Children's last retreat,
They called it, the Pied Piper's Street, —
Where any one playing on pipe or tabor
Was sure for the future to lose his labor.
Nor suffered they Hostelry or Tavern
   To shock with mirth a street so solemn ;.
But opposite the place of the cavern
   They wrote the story on a column,
And on the Great Church Window painted
The same, to make the world acquainted
How their children were stolen away ;
And there it stands to this very day.
And I must not omit to say
That in Transylvania there 's a tribe
Of alien people that ascribe
The outlandish ways and dress
On which their neighbors lay such stress,
To their fathers and mothers having risen
Out of some subterraneous prison
Into which they were trepanned
Long time ago in a mighty band
Out of Hamelin town in Brunswick land,
But how or why, they don't understand.

So, Willy, let you and me be wipers
Of scores out with all men — especially pipers :
And, whether they pipe us free from rats or from mice,
If we 've promised them aught, let us keep our promise.

FAME.

SEE, as the prettiest graves will do in time,
  Our poet's wants the freshness of its prime;
Spite of the sexton's browsing horse, the sods
Have struggled through its binding osier-rods;
Headstone and half-sunk footstone lean awry,
Wanting the brickwork promised by and by;
How the minute gray lichens, plate o'er plate,
Have softened down the crisp-cut name and date!

LOVE.

SO, the year 's done with!
  (*Love me forever!*)
All March begun with,
  April's endeavor;
May-wreaths that bound me
  June needs must sever!
Now snows fall round me,
  Quenching June's fever, —
  (*Love me forever!*)

SONG.

NAY but you, who do not love her,
  Is she not pure gold, my mistress?
Holds earth aught, — speak truth, — above her?
Aught like this tress, see, and this tress,

And this last fairest tress of all
So fair, see, ere I let it fall!

Because, you spend your lives in praising;
   To praise, you search the wide world over;
So, why not witness, calmly gazing,
   If earth holds aught — speak truth — above her?
Above this tress, and this I touch
But cannot praise, I love so much!

INCIDENT OF THE FRENCH CAMP.

YOU know, we French stormed Ratisbon:
   A mile or so away
On a little mound, Napoléon
   Stood on our storming-day;
With neck out-thrust, you fancy how,
   Legs wide, arms locked behind,
As if to balance the prone brow
   Oppressive with its mind.

Just as perhaps he mused, "My plans
   That soar, to earth may fall,
Let once my army-leader, Lannes,
   Waver at yonder wall," —
Out 'twixt the battery-smokes there flew
   A rider, bound on bound
Full-galloping; nor bridle drew
   Until he reached the mound.

Then off there flung in smiling joy,
   And held himself erect
By just his horse's mane, a boy:
   You hardly could suspect —

4

(So tight he kept his lips compressed,
　　Scarce any blood came through)
You looked twice ere you saw his breast
　　Was all but shot in two.

" Well," cried he, " Emperor, by God's grace
　　We 've got you Ratisbon !
The Marshal 's in the market-place,
　　And you 'll be there anon

To see your flag-bird flap his vans
  Where I, to heart's desire,
Perched him!" The Chief's eye flashed; his plans
  Soared up again like fire.

The Chief's eye flashed; but presently
  Softened itself, as sheathes
A film the mother eagle's eye
  When her bruised eaglet breathes:
"You're wounded!" "Nay," his soldier's pride
  Touched to the quick, he said:
"I 'm killed, Sire!" And, his Chief beside,
  Smiling, the boy fell dead.

THE BOY AND THE ANGEL.

MORNING, evening, noon, and night,
  "Praise God," sang Theocrite.

Then to his poor trade he turned,
By which the daily meal was earned.

Hard he labored, long and well;
O'er his work the boy's curls fell:

But ever, at each period,
He stopped and sang, "Praise God."

Then back again his curls he threw,
And cheerful turned to work anew.

Said Blaise, the listening monk, "Well done;
I doubt not thou art heard, my son:

" As well as if thy voice to-day
Were praising God, the Pope's great way.

" This Easter Day, the Pope at Rome
Praises God from Peter's dome."

Said Theocrite, " Would God that I
Might praise Him, that great way, and die ! "

Night passed, day shone,
And Theocrite was gone.

With God a day endures alway,
A thousand years are but a day.

God said in Heaven, " Nor day nor night
Now brings the voice of my delight."

Then Gabriel, like a rainbow's birth,
Spread his wings and sank to earth ;

Entered in flesh, the empty cell,
Lived there, and played the craftsman well :

And morning, evening, noon, and night,
Praised God in place of Theocrite.

And from a boy, to youth he grew :
The man put off the stripling's hue :

The man matured and fell away
Into the season of decay :

And ever o'er the trade he bent,
And ever lived on earth content.

(He did God's will ; to him, all one
If on the earth or in the sun.)

God said, " A praise is in mine ear ;
There is no doubt in it, no fear :

"So sing old worlds, and so
New worlds that from my footstool go.

"Clearer loves sound other ways:
I miss my little human praise."

Then forth sprang Gabriel's wings, off fell
The flesh disguise, remained the cell.

'T was Easter Day: he flew to Rome,
And paused above Saint Peter's dome.

In the tiring-room close by
The great outer gallery,

With his holy vestments dight,
Stood the new Pope, Theocrite

And all his past career
Came back upon him clear,

Since when, a boy, he plied his trade,
Till on his life the sickness weighed;

And in his cell, when death drew near,
An angel in a dream brought cheer;

And rising from the sickness drear
He grew a priest, and now stood here.

To the East with praise he turned,
And on his sight the angel burned.

"I bore thee from thy craftsman's cell,
And set thee here; I did not well.

"Vainly I left my angel's-sphere,
Vain was thy dream of many a year.

"Thy voice's praise seemed weak; it dropped, —
Creation's chorus stopped!

" Go back and praise again
The early way, — while I remain.

" With that weak voice of our disdain,
Take up Creation's pausing strain.

" Back to the cell and poor employ :
Become the craftsman and the boy ! "

Theocrite grew old at home ;
A new Pope dwelt in Peter's Dome.

One vanished as the other died :
They sought God side by side.

TIME'S REVENGES.

I 'VE a Friend, over the sea ;
I like him, but he loves me ;
It all grew out of the books I write ;
They find such favor in his sight
That he slaughters you with savage looks
Because you don't admire my books :
He does himself though, — and if some vein
Were to snap to-night in this heavy brain,
To-morrow month, if I lived to try,
Round should I just turn quietly,
Or out of the bedclothes stretch my hand
Till I found him, come from his foreign land
To be my nurse in this poor place,
And make me broth and wash my face,
And light my fire, and, all the while,
Bear with his old good-humored smile
That I told him, " Better have kept away

Than come and kill me, night and day,
With worse than fever's throbs and shoots,
At the creaking of his clumsy boots."
I am as sure that this he would do,
As that St. Paul's is striking Two :
And I think I had rather . . . woe is me
— Yes, rather see him than not see,
If lifting a hand would seat him there
Before me in the empty chair
To-night, when my head aches indeed,
And I can neither think, nor read,
And these blue fingers will not hold
The pen ; this garret 's freezing cold!

And I 've a Lady — There he wakes,
The laughing fiend and prince of snakes
Within me, at her name, to pray
Fate send some creature in the way
Of my love for her, to be down-torn,
Upthrust and onward borne
So I might prove myself that sea
Of passion which I needs must be !
Call my thoughts false and my fancies quaint,
And my style infirm, and its figures faint,
All the critics say, and more blame yet,
And not one angry word you get !
But, please you, wonder I would put
My cheek beneath that Lady's foot
Rather than trample under mine
The laurels of the Florentine,
And you shall see how the Devil spends
A fire God gave for other ends !
I tell you, I stride up and down
This garret, crowned with love's best crown,
And feasted with love's perfect feast,
To think I kill for her, at least,
Body and soul and peace and fame,
Alike youth's end and manhood's aim,
— So is my spirit, as flesh with sin,

Filled full, eaten out and in
With the face of her, the eyes of her,
The lips and little chin, the stir
Of shadow round her mouth; and she
— I 'll tell you — calmly would decree
That I should roast at a slow fire,
If that would compass her desire
And make her one whom they invite
To the famous ball to-morrow night.

There may be Heaven; there must be Hell;
Meantime, there is our Earth here, — well!

THE GLOVE.

"HEIGH-HO!" yawned one day King Francis,
        "Distance all value enhances!
When a man 's busy, why, leisure
Strikes him as wonderful pleasure.
'Faith, and at leisure once is he?
Straightway he wants to be busy.
Here we 've got peace; and aghast I 'm
Caught thinking war the true pastime!
Is there a reason in metre?
Give us your speech, master Peter!"
I who, if mortal dare say so,
Ne'er am at loss with my Naso,
"Sire," I replied, "joys prove cloudlets:
Men are the merest Ixions," —
Here the King whistled aloud, "Let 's
. . . Heigh-ho . . . go look at our lions!"
Such are the sorrowful chances
If you talk fine to King Francis.

And so, to the court-yard proceeding,
Our company, Francis was leading,
Increased by new followers tenfold   .
Before he arrived at the penfold ;
Lords, ladies, like clouds which bedizen
At sunset the western horizon.
And Sir De Lorge pressed 'mid the foremost
With the dame he professed to adore most, —
O, what a face !   One by fits eyed
Her, and the horrible pitside ;
For the penfold surrounded a hollow
Which led where the eye scarce dared follow,
And shelved to the chamber secluded
Where Bluebeard, the great lion, brooded.
The King hailed his keeper, an Arab
As glossy and black as a scarab,
And bade him make sport and at once stir
Up and out of his den the old monster.
They opened a hole in the wire-work
Across it, and dropped there a firework,
And fled ; one's heart's beating redoubled ;
A pause, while the pit's mouth was troubled,
The blackness and silence so utter,   .
By the firework's slow sparkling and sputter ;
Then earth in a sudden contortion
Gave out to our gaze her abortion !
Such a brute !   Were I friend Clement Marot
(Whose experience of nature 's but narrow,
And whose faculties move in no small mist
When he versifies David the Psalmist)
I should study that brute to describe you
Illum Juda Leonem de Tribu !
One's whole blood grew curdling and creepy
To see the black mane, vast and heapy,
The tail in the air stiff and straining,
The wide eyes, nor waxing nor waning,
As over the barrier which bounded
His platform, and us who surrounded
The barrier, they reached and they rested

On the space that might stand him in best stead :
For who knew, he thought, what the amazement,
The eruption of clatter and blaze meant,
And if, in this minute of wonder,
No outlet, 'mid lightning and thunder,
Lay broad, and, his shackles all shivered,
The lion at last was delivered ?
Ay, that was the open sky o'erhead !
And you saw by the flash on his forehead,
By the hope in those eyes wide and steady,
He was leagues in the desert already,
Driving the flocks up the mountain,
Or catlike couched hard by the fountain
To waylay the date-gathering negress :
So guarded he entrance or egress.
" How he stands ! " quoth the King : " we may well swear,
No novice, we 've won our spurs elsewhere,
And so can afford the confession,
We exercise wholesome discretion
In keeping aloof from his threshold ;
Once hold you, those jaws want no fresh hold,
Their first would too pleasantly purloin
The visitor's brisket or surloin :
But who 's he would prove so foolhardy ?
Not the best man of Marignan, pardie ! "

The sentence no sooner was uttered,
Than over the rails a glove fluttered,
Fell close to the lion, and rested :
The dame 't was, who flung it and jested
With life so, De Lorge had been wooing
For months past ; he sat there pursuing
His suit, weighing out with nonchalance
Fine speeches like gold from a balance.

Sound the trumpet, no true knight 's a tarrier !
De Lorge made one leap at the barrier,
Walked straight to the glove, — while the lion
Ne'er moved, kept his far-reaching eye on

The palm-tree-edged desert-spring's sapphire,
And the musky oiled skin of the Kaffir, —
Picked it up, and as calmly retreated,
Leaped back where the lady was seated,
And full in the face of its owner
Flung the glove, —

                        " Your heart's queen, you dethrone her ?
So should I," —cried the King, — " 't was mere vanity,
Not love, set that task to humanity ! "
Lords and ladies alike turned with loathing
From such a proved wolf in sheep's clothing.
Not so, I; for I caught an expression
In her brow's undisturbed self-possession
Amid the Court's scoffing and merriment, —
As if from no pleasing experiment
She rose, yet of pain nót much heedful
So long as the process was needful, —
As if she had tried in a crucible,
To what " speeches like gold," were reducible,
And, finding the finest prove copper,
Felt the smoke in her face was but proper ;
To know what she had *not* to trust to,
Was worth all the ashes, and dust too.
She went out 'mid hooting and laughter ;
Clement Marot stayed ; I followed after,
And asked, as a grace, what it all meant, —
If she wished not the rash deed's recalment ?
" For I," — so I spoke, — " am a Poet :
Human nature, — behooves that I know it ! "

She told me, " Too long had I heard
Of the deed proved alone by the word :
For my love, — what De Lorge would not dare !
With my scorn, — what De Lorge could compare !
And the endless descriptions of death
He would brave when my lip formed a breath,
I must reckon as braved, or, of course,
Doubt his word, — and moreover, perforce,

For such gifts as no lady could spurn,
Must offer my love in return.
When I looked on your lion, it brought
All the dangers at once to my thought,
Encountered by all sorts of men,
Before he was lodged in his den, —
From the poor slave whose club or bare hands
Dug the trap, set the snare on the sands,
With no King and no Court to applaud,
By no shame, should he shrink, overawed,
Yet to capture the creature made shift,
That his rude boys might laugh at the gift,
To the page who last leaped o'er the fence
Of the pit, on no greater pretence
Than to get back the bonnet he dropped,
Lest his pay for a week should be stopped, —
So, wiser I judged it to make
One trial what ' death for my sake '
Really meant, while the power was yet mine,
Than to wait until time should define
Such a phrase not so simply as I,
Who took it to mean just ' to die.'
The blow a glove gives is but weak, —
Does the mark yet discolor my cheek ?
But when the heart suffers a blow,
Will the pain pass so soon, do you know ? "

I looked, as away she was sweeping,
And saw a youth eagerly keeping
As close as he dared to the doorway :
No doubt that a noble should more weigh
His life than befits a plebeian ;
And yet, had our brute been Nemean, —
(I judge by a certain calm fervor
The youth stepped with, forward to serve her)
— He 'd have scarce thought you did him the worst turn
If you whispered "Friend, what you 'd get, first earn ! "
And when, shortly after, she carried
Her shame from the Court, and they married,

To that marriage some happiness, maugre
The voice of the Court, I dared augur.

For De Lorge, he made women with men vie,
Those in wonder and praise, these in envy;
And in short stood so plain a head taller
That he wooed and won . . . How do you call her?
The beauty, that rose in the sequel
To the King's love, who loved her a week well;
And 't was noticed he never would honor
De Lorge (who looked daggers upon her)
With the easy commission of stretching
His legs in the service, and fetching
His wife, from her chamber, those straying
Sad gloves she was always mislaying,
While the King took the closet to chat in, —
But of course this adventure came pat in;
And never the King told the story,
How bringing a glove brought such glory,
But the wife smiled, — "His nerves are grown firmer, —
Mine he brings now and utters no murmur!"

"HOW THEY BROUGHT THE GOOD NEWS FROM GHENT TO AIX."

I SPRANG to the stirrup, and Joris, and he;
I galloped, Dirck galloped, we galloped all three;
"Good speed!" cried the watch, as the gate-bolts undrew;
"Speed!" echoed the wall to us galloping through;
Behind shut the postern, the lights sank to rest,
And into the midnight we galloped abreast.

Not a word to each other; we kept the great pace
Neck by neck, stride by stride, never changing our place;

I turned in my saddle and made its girths tight,
Then shortened each stirrup, and set the pique right,
Rebuckled the check-strap, chained slacker the bit,
Nor galloped less steadily Roland a whit.

'T was moonset at starting; but while we drew near
Lokeren, the cocks crew and twilight dawned clear;
At Boom, a great yellow star came out to see;
At Düffeld, 't was morning as plain as could be;
And from Mecheln church-steeple we heard the half-chime,
So Joris broke silence with, " Yet there is time! "

At Aerschot, up leaped of a sudden the sun,
And against him the cattle stood black every one,
To stare through the mist at us galloping past,
And I saw my stout galloper Roland at last,
With resolute shoulders, each butting away
The haze, as some bluff river headland its spray.

And his low head and crest, just one sharp ear bent back
For my voice, and the other pricked out on his track;
And one eye's black intelligence, — ever that glance
O'er its white edge at me, his own master, askance!
And the thick heavy spume-flakes which aye and anon
His fierce lips shook upwards in galloping on.

By Hasselt, Dirck groaned; and cried Joris, " Stay spur!
Your Roos galloped bravely, the fault 's not in her,
We 'll remember at Aix," — for one heard the quick wheeze
Of her chest, saw the stretched neck and staggering knees,
And sunk tail, and horrible heave of the flank,
As down on her haunches she shuddered and sank.

So we were left galloping, Joris and I,
Past Looz and past Tongres, no cloud in the sky;
The broad sun above laughed a pitiless laugh,
'Neath our feet broke the brittle bright stubble like chaff;
Till over by Dalhem a dome-spire sprang white,
And " Gallop," gasped Joris, " for Aix is in sight! "

" How they 'll greet us ! " — and all in a moment his roan
Rolled neck and croup over, lay dead as a stone ;
And there was my Roland to bear the whole weight
Of the news which alone could save Aix from her fate,
With his nostrils like pits full of blood to the brim,
And with circles of red for his eye-sockets' rim.

Then I cast loose my buff-coat, each holster let fall,
Shook off both my jack-boots, let go belt and all,

Stood up in the stirrup, leaned, patted his ear,
Called my Roland his pet-name, my horse without peer;
Clapped my hands, laughed and sang, any noise, bad or good,
Till at length into Aix Roland galloped and stood.

And all I remember is, friends flocking round
As I sat with his head 'twixt my knees on the ground,
And no voice but was praising this Roland of mine,
As I poured down his throat our last measure of wine,
Which (the burgesses voted by common consent)
Was no more than his due who brought good news from Ghent.

LOVE AMONG THE RUINS.

WHERE the quiet-colored end of evening smiles
        Miles and miles
On the solitary pastures where our sheep,
        Half-asleep,
Tinkle homeward through the twilight, stray or stop
        As they crop, —

Was the site once of a city great and gay,
        (So they say)
Of our country's very capital, its prince
        Ages since
Held his court in, gathered councils, wielding far
        Peace or war.

Now, — the country does not even boast a tree,
        As you see,
To distinguish slopes of verdure, certain rills
        From the hills
Intersect and give a name to, (else they run
        Into one)

Where the domed·and daring palace shot its spires
   Up like fires
O'er the hundred-gated circuit of a wall
   Bounding all,
Made of marble, men might march on nor be prest,
   Twelve abreast.

And such plenty and perfection, see, of grass
   Never was !
Such a carpet as, this summer-time, o'erspreads
   And embeds
Every vestige of the city, guessed alone,
   Stock or stone —

Where a multitude of men breathed joy and woe
   Long ago ;
Lust of glory pricked their hearts up, dread of shame
   Struck them tame ; ·
And that glory and that shame alike, the gold
   Bought and sold.

Now, — the single little turret that remains
   On the plains,
By the caper overrooted, by the gourd
   Overscored,
While the patching houseleek's head of blossom winks
   Through the chinks —

Marks the basement whence a tower in ancient time
   Sprang sublime,
And a burning ring all round, the chariots traced
   As they raced,
And the monarch and his minions and his dames
   Viewed the games.

And I know, while thus the quiet-colored eve
   Smiles to leave
To their folding, all our many-tinkling fleece
   In such peace,
5

And the slopes and rills in undistinguished gray
            Melt away —

That a girl with eager eyes and yellow hair
            Waits me there
In the turret, whence the charioteers caught soul
            For the goal,
When the king looked, where she looks now, breathless, dumb,
            Till I come.

But he looked upon the city, every side,
            Far and wide,
All the mountains topped with temples, all the glades'
            Colonnades,
All the causeys, bridges, aqueducts, — and then,
            All the men!

When I do come, she will speak not, she will stand,
            Either hand
On my shoulder, give her eyes the first embrace
            Of my face,
Ere we rush, ere we extinguish sight and speech
            Each on each.

In one year they sent a million fighters forth
            South and north,
And they built their gods a brazen pillar high
            As the sky,
Yet reserved a thousand chariots in full force, —
            Gold, of course.

O heart! O blood that freezes, blood that burns!
            Earth's returns
For whole centuries of folly, noise, and sin!
            Shut them in,
With their triumphs and their glories and the rest.
            Love is best!

A WOMAN'S LAST WORD.

LET 'S contend no more, Love,
　　Strive nor weep, —
All be as before, Love,
　　— Only sleep!

What so wild as words are?
　　— I and thou
In debate, as birds are,
　　Hawk on bough!

See the creature stalking
　　While we speak, —
Hush and hide the talking,
　　Cheek on cheek!

What so false as truth is,
　　False to thee?
Where the serpent's tooth is,
　　Shun the tree, —

Where the apple reddens
　　Never pry, —
Lest we lose our Edens,
　　Eve and I!

Be a god and hold me
　　With a charm, —
Be a man and fold me
　　With thine arm!

Teach me, only teach, Love!
　　As I ought
I will speak thy speech, Love,
　　Think thy thought, —

Meet, if thou require it,
  Both demands,
Laying flesh and spirit
  In thy hands!

That shall be to-morrow
  Not to-night:
I must bury sorrow
  Out of sight.

— Must a little weep, Love,
  — Foolish me!
And so fall asleep, Love,
  Loved by thee.

A SERENADE AT THE VILLA.

THAT was I, you heard last night
    When there rose no moon at all,
Nor, to pierce the strained and tight
    Tent of heaven, a planet small:
Life was dead, and so was light.

Not a twinkle from the fly,
    Not a glimmer from the worm.
When the crickets stopped their cry,
    When the owls forbore a term,
You heard music; that was I.

Earth turned in her sleep with pain,
    Sultrily suspired for proof:
In at heaven and out again,
    Lightning! — where it broke the roof,
Bloodlike, some few drops of rain.

What they could my words expressed,
    O my love, my all, my one!
Singing helped the verses best,
    And when singing's best was done,
To my lute I left the rest.

So wore night; the east was gray,
    White the broad-faced hemlock flowers;
Soon would come another day;
    Ere its first of heavy hours
Found me, I had past away.

What became of all the hopes,
    Words and song and lute as well?
Say, this struck you, — " When life gropes
    Feebly for the path where fell
Light last on the evening slopes,

"One friend in that path shall be
    To secure my steps from wrong;
One to count night day for me,
    Patient through the watches long,
Serving most with none to see."

Never say, — as something bodes, —
    "So the worst has yet a worse!
When life halts 'neath double loads,
    Better the task-master's curse
Than such music on the roads!

"When no moon succeeds the sun,
    Nor can pierce the midnight's tent
Any star, the smallest one,
    While some drops, where lightning went,
Show the final storm begun, —

"When the fire-fly hides its spot,
    When the garden-voices fail
In the darkness thick and hot, —

Shall another voice avail,
That shape be where those are not?

" Has some plague a longer lease
    Proffering its help uncouth?
Can't one even die in peace?
    As one shuts one's eyes on youth,
Is that face the last one sees?"

O, how dark your villa was,
    Windows fast and obdurate!
How the garden grudged me grass
    Where I stood, — the iron gate
Ground its teeth to let me pass!

EVELYN HOPE.

BEAUTIFUL Evelyn Hope is dead!   .
    Sit and watch by her side an hour.
That is her book-shelf, this her bed;
    She plucked that piece of geranium-flower,
Beginning to die too, in the glass.
    Little has yet been changed, I think, —
The shutters are shut, no light may pass
    Save two long rays through the hinge's chink.

Sixteen years old when she died!
    Perhaps she had scarcely heard my name,
It was not her time to love: beside,
    Her life had many a hope and aim,
Duties enough and little cares,
    And now was quiet, now astir, —
Till God's hand beckoned unawares,
    And the sweet white brow is all of her.

Is it too late then, Evelyn Hope?
  What, your soul was pure and true,
The good stars met in your horoscope,
  Made you of spirit, fire, and dew, —
And just because I was thrice as old,
  And our paths in the world diverged so wide,
Each was naught to each, must I be told?
  We were fellow-mortals, naught beside?

No, indeed! for God above
  Is great to grant, as mighty to make,
And creates the love to reward the love, —
  I claim you still, for my own love's sake!
Delayed it may be for more lives yet,
  Through worlds I shall traverse, not a few, —
Much is to learn and much to forget
  Ere the time be come for taking you.

But the time will come, — at last it will,
  When, Evelyn Hope, what meant, I shall say,
In the lower earth, in the years long still,
  That body and soul so pure and gay?
Why your hair was amber, I shall divine,
  And your mouth of your own geranium's red, —
And what you would do with me, in fine,
  In the new life come in the old one's stead.

I have lived, I shall say, so much since then,
  Given up myself so many times,
Gained me the gains of various men,
  Ransacked the ages, spoiled the climes;

Yet one thing, one, in my soul's full scope,
  Either I missed or itself missed me, —
And I want and find you, Evelyn Hope!
  What is the issue? let us see!

I loved you, Evelyn, all the while;
  My heart seemed full as it could hold, —
There was place and to spare for the frank young smile,
  And the red young mouth, and the hair's young gold.
So, hush, — I will give you this leaf to keep, —
  See, I shut it inside the sweet cold hand.
There, that is our secret! go to sleep;
  You will wake, and remember, and understand.

MY STAR.

ALL that I know
    Of a certain star,
  Is, it can throw
    (Like the angled spar)
  Now a dart of red,
    Now a dart of blue,
  Till my friends have said
    They would fain see, too,
My star that dartles the red and the blue!
Then it stops like a bird, — like a flower, hangs furled;
  They must solace themselves with the Saturn above it.
What matter to me if their star is a world?
  Mine has opened its soul to me; therefore I love it.

LOVE IN ·A LIFE.

ROOM after room,
   I hunt the house through
We inhabit together.
Heart, fear nothing, for, heart, thou shalt find her,
Next time, herself! — not the trouble behind her
Left in the curtain, the couch's perfume!
As she brushed it, the cornice-wreath blossomed anew,—
Yon looking-glass gleamed at the wave of her feather.

Yet the day wears,
And door succeeds door;
I try the fresh fortune, —
Range the wide house from the wing to the centre.
Still the same chance! she goes out as I enter.
Spend my whole day in the quest, — who cares?
But 't is twilight, you see, — with such suites to explore,
Such closets to search, such alcoves to importune!

LIFE IN A LOVE.

ESCAPE me?
   Never,
Beloved!
While I am I, and you are you,
  So long as the world contains us both,
  Me the loving and you the loth,
While the one eludes, must the other pursue.
My life is a fault at last, I fear, —
  It seems too much like a fate, indeed!

Though I do my best I shall scarce succeed, —
But what if I fail of my purpose here ?
It is but to keep the nerves at strain,
　　To dry one's eyes and laugh at a fall,
And baffled, get up to begin again, —
　　So the chace takes up one's life, that's all.
While, look but once from your furthest bound,
　　At me so deep in the dust and dark,
No sooner the old hope drops to ground
　　Than a new one, straight to the selfsame mark,
　　　　　　I shape me, —
　　　　　　Ever
　　　　　　Removed !

MEMORABILIA.

AH, did you once see Shelley plain,
　　And did he stop and speak to you ?
And did you speak to him again ?
　　How strange it seems, and new !

But you were living before that,
　　And you are living after,
And the memory I started at, —
　　My starting moves your laughter !

I crossed a moor with a name of its own
　　And a use in the world no doubt,
Yet a hand's-breadth of it shines alone
　　'Mid the blank miles round about, —

For there I picked up on the heather
　　And there I put inside my breast
A moulted feather, an eagle-feather, —
　　Well, I forget the rest.

AFTER.

TAKE the cloak from his face, and at first
    Let the corpse do its worst.

How he lies in his rights of a man!
    Death has done all death can.
And, absorbed in the new life he leads,
    He recks not, he heeds
Nor his wrong nor my vengeance, — both strike
    On his senses alike,
And are lost in the solemn and strange
    Surprise of the change.
Ha, what avails death to erase
    His offence, my disgrace?
I would we were boys as of old
    In the field, by the fold, —
His outrage, God's patience, man's scorn
    Were so easily borne.

I stand here now, he lies in his place, —
    Cover the face.

IN THREE DAYS.

SO, I shall see her in three days
    And just one night, but nights are short,
Then two long hours, and that is morn.
See how I come, unchanged, unworn, —
Feel, where my life broke off from thine,
How fresh the splinters keep and fine, —
Only a touch and we combine!

Too long, this time of year, the days!
But nights — at least the nights are short.
As night shows where her one moon is,
A hand's-breadth of pure light and bliss,
So, life's night gives my lady birth
And my eyes hold her! what is worth
The rest of heaven, the rest of earth?

O loaded curls, release your store
Of warmth and scent as once before
The tingling hair did, lights and darks
Out-breaking into fairy sparks
When under curl and curl I pried
After the warmth and scent inside
Through lights and darks how manifold, —
The dark inspired, the light controlled!
As early Art embrowned the gold.

What great fear — should one say, " Three days
That change the world, might change as well
Your fortune; and if joy delays,
Be happy that no worse befell."
What small fear — if another says,
" Three days and one short night beside
May throw no shadow on your ways;
But years must teem with change untried,
With chance not easily defied,
With an end somewhere undescried."
No fear! — or if a fear be born
This minute, it dies out in scorn.
Fear?   I shall see her in three days
And one night, now the nights are short,
Then just two hours, and that is morn.

IN A YEAR.

NEVER any more
　　While I live,
Need I hope to see his face
　　As before.
Once his love grown chill,
　　Mine may strive, —
Bitterly we re-embrace,
　　Single still.

Was it something said,
　　Something done,
Vexed him? was it touch of hand,
　　Turn of head?
Strange! that very way
　　Love begun.
I as little understand
　　Love's decay.

When I sewed or drew,
  I recall
How he looked as if I sang,
  — Sweetly too.
If I spoke a word,
  First of all
Up his cheek the color sprang,
  Then he heard.

Sitting by my side,
  At my feet,
So he breathed the air I breathed,
  Satisfied !
I, too, at love's brim
  Touched the sweet :
I would die if death bequeathed
  Sweet to him.

" Speak, I love thee best ! "
  He exclaimed.
" Let thy love my own foretell," —
  I confessed :
" Clasp my heart on thine
  Now unblamed,
Since upon thy soul as well
  Hangeth mine ! "

Was it wrong to own,
  Being truth ?
Why should all the giving prove
  His alone ?
I had wealth and ease,
  Beauty, youth, —
Since my lover gave me love,
  I gave these.

That was all I meant,
  — To be just,
And the passion I had raised
  To content.

Since he chose to change
   Gold for dust,
If I gave him what he praised
   Was it strange?

Would he loved me yet,
   On and on,
While I found some way undreamed
   — Paid my debt!
Gave more life and more,
   Till, all gone,
He should smile, " She never seemed
   Mine before.

" What, — she felt the while,
   Must I think?
Love 's so different with us men,"
   He should smile.
" Dying for my sake, —
   White and pink!
Can't we touch these bubbles then
   But they break? "

Dear, the pang is brief.
   Do thy part,
Have thy pleasure. How perplext
   Grows belief!
Well, this cold clay clod
   Was man's heart.
Crumble it, — and what comes next?
   Is it God?

"DE GUSTIBUS —"

YOUR ghost will walk, you lover of trees,
    (If loves remain)
     In an English lane,
By a cornfield-side a-flutter with poppies.
Hark, those two in the hazel coppice, —
A boy and a girl, if the good fates please,
    Making love, say, —
    The happier they!
Draw yourself up from the light of the moon,
And let them pass, as they will too soon,
    With the bean-flowers' boon,
    And the blackbird's tune,
    And May, and June!

What I love best in all the world,
Is, a castle, precipice-encurled,
In a gash of the wind-grieved Apennine.
Or look for me, old fellow of mine
(If I get my head from out the mouth
O' the grave, and loose my spirit's bands,
And come again to the land of lands), —
In a seaside house to the farther south,
Where the baked cicalas die of drouth,
And one sharp tree ('t is a cypress) stands,
By the many hundred years red-rusted,
Rough iron-spiked, ripe fruit-o'ercrusted,
My sentinel to guard the sands
To the water's edge.   For,.what expands
Without the house, but the great opaque
Blue breadth of sea, and not a break?
While, in the house, forever crumbles
Some fragment of the frescoed walls,
From blisters where a scorpion sprawls.
A girl barefooted brings and tumbles

Down on the pavement, green-flesh melons,
And says there 's news to-day, — the king
Was shot at, touched in the liver-wing,
Goes with his Bourbon arm in a sling.
— She hopes they have not caught the felons.
　　Italy, my Italy !
Queen Mary's saying serves for me, —
　　(When fortune's malice
　　Lost her, Calais.)
Open my heart and you will see
Graved inside of it, "Italy."
Such lovers old are I and she ;
So it always was, so it still shall be !

WOMEN AND ROSES.

I DREAM of a red-rose tree.
　And which of its roses three
Is the dearest rose to me ?

Round and round, like a dance of snow
In a dazzling drift, as its guardians, go
Floating the women faded for ages,
Sculptured in stone, on the poet's pages.
Then follow the women fresh and gay,
Living and loving and loved to-day.
Last, in the rear, flee the multitude of maidens,
Beauties unborn. And all, to one cadence,
They circle their rose on my rose-tree.

　　Dear rose, thy term is reached,
　　Thy leaf hangs loose and bleached :
　　Bees pass it unimpeached.
6

Stay then, stoop, since I cannot climb,
You, great shapes of the antique time !
How shall I fix you, fire you, freeze you,
Break my heart at your feet to please you ?
O to possess, and be possessed !
Hearts that beat 'neath each pallid breast !
But once of love, the poesy, the passion,
Drink once and die ! — In vain, the same fashion,
They circle their rose on my rose-tree.

> Dear rose, thy joy 's undimmed ;
> Thy cup is ruby-rimmed,
> Thy cup's heart nectar-brimmed.

Deep as drops from a statue's plinth
The bee sucked in by the hyacinth,
So will I bury me while burning,
Quench like him at a plunge my yearning,
Eyes in your eyes, lips on your lips !
Fold me fast where the cincture slips,
Prison all my soul in eternities of pleasure !
Girdle me once !   But no, — in their old measure
They circle their rose on my rose-tree.

> Dear rose without a thorn,
> Thy bud 's the babe unborn,
> First streak of a new morn.

Wings, lend wings for the cold, the clear !
What 's far conquers what is near.
Roses will bloom nor want beholders,
Sprung from the dust where our own flesh moulders.
What shall arrive with the cycle's change ?
A novel grace and a beauty strange.
I will make an Eve, be the artist that began her,
Shaped her to his mind ! — Alas ! in like manner
They circle their rose on my rose-tree.

THE GUARDIAN-ANGEL:

A PICTURE AT FANO.

DEAR and great Angel, wouldst thou only leave
    That child, when thou hast done with him, for me!
Let me sit all the day here, that when eve
    Shall find performed thy special ministry
And time come for departure, thou, suspending
Thy flight, may'st see another child for tending,
    Another still, to quiet and retrieve.

Then I shall feel thee step one step, no more,
    From where thou standest now, to where I gaze,
And suddenly my head be covered o'er
    With those wings, white above the child who prays
Now on that tomb, — and I shall feel thee guarding
Me, out of all the world; for me, discarding
    Yon heaven thy home, that waits and opes its door!

I would not look up thither past thy head
    Because the door opes, like that child, I know,
For I should have thy gracious face instead,
    Thou bird of God! And wilt thou bend me low
Like him, and lay, like his, my hands together,
And lift them up to pray, and gently tether
    Me, as thy lamb there, with thy garment's spread?

If this was ever granted, I would rest
    My head beneath thine, while thy healing hands
Close-covered both my eyes beside thy breast,
    Pressing the brain, which too much thought expands,
Back to its proper size again, and smoothing
Distortion down till every nerve had soothing,
    And all lay quiet, happy, and supprest.

How soon all worldly wrong would be repaired!
  I think how I should view the earth and skies
And sea, when once again my brow was bared
  After thy healing, with such different eyes.
O world, as God has made it! all is beauty:
And knowing this, is love, and love is duty.
  What further may be sought for or declared?

Guercino drew this angel I saw teach
  (Alfred, dear friend,) — that little child to pray,
Holding the little hands up, each to each
  Pressed gently, — with his own head turned away
Over the earth where so much lay before him
Of work to do, though heaven was opening o'er him,
  And he was left at Fano by the beach.

We were at Fano, and three times we went
  To sit and see him in his chapel there,
And drink his beauty to our soul's content,
  — My angel with me too: and since I care
For dear Guercino's fame, (to which in power
And glory comes this picture for a dower,
  Fraught with a pathos so magnificent,)

And since he did not work so earnestly
  At all times, and has else endured some wrong, —
I took one thought his picture struck from me,
  And spread it out, translating it to song.
My Love is here. Where are you, dear old friend?
How rolls the Wairoa at your world's far end?
  This is Ancona, yonder is the sea.

TWO IN THE CAMPAGNA.

I WONDER do you feel to-day
    As I have felt, since, hand in hand,
We sat down on the grass, to stray
    In spirit better through the land,
This morn of Rome and May?

For me, I touched a thought, I know,
    Has tantalized me many times,
(Like turns of thread the spiders throw
    Mocking across our path) for rhymes
To catch at and let go.

Help me to hold it: first it left
    The yellowing fennel, run to seed
There, branching from the brickwork's cleft,
    Some old tomb's ruin: yonder weed
Took up the floating weft,

Where one small orange cup amassed
    Five beetles, — blind and green they grope
Among the honey-meal, — and last
    Everywhere on the grassy slope
I traced it. Hold it fast!

The champaign with its endless fleece
    Of feathery grasses everywhere!
Silence and passion, joy and peace,
    An everlasting wash of air, —
Rome's ghost since her decease.

Such life there, through such lengths of hours,
    Such miracles performed in play,
Such primal naked forms of flowers,
    Such letting Nature have her way
While Heaven looks from its towers.

How say you?   Let us, O my dove,
　　Let us be unashamed of soul,
As earth lies bare to heaven above.
　　How is it under our control
To love or not to love?

I would that you were all to me,
　　You that are just so much, no more,—
Nor yours, nor mine,—nor slave, nor free!
　　Where does the fault lie? what the core
Of the wound, since wound must be?

I would I could adopt your will,
　　See with your eyes, and set my heart
Beating by yours, and drink my fill
　　At your soul's springs,—your part, my part
In life, for good and ill.

No.   I yearn upward,—touch you close,
　　Then stand away.   I kiss your cheek,
Catch your soul's warmth,—I pluck the rose
　　And love it more than tongue can speak,—
Then the good minute goes.

Already how am I so far
　　Out of that minute?   Must I go
Still like the thistle-ball, no bar,
　　Onward, whenever light winds blow,
Fixed by no friendly star?

Just when I seemed about to learn!
　　Where is the thread now?   Off again!
The old trick!   Only I discern—
　　Infinite passion and the pain
Of finite hearts that yearn.

THE PATRIOT.

AN OLD STORY.

I T was roses, roses, all the way,
   With myrtle mixed in my path like mad.
The house-roofs seemed to heave and sway,
   The church-spires flamed, such flags they had,
A year ago on this very day!

The air broke into a mist with bells,
   The old walls rocked with the crowds and cries.
Had I said, " Good folks, mere noise repels, —
   But give me your sun from yonder skies! "
They had answered, " And afterward, what else? "

Alack, it was I who leaped at the sun,
   To give it my loving friends to keep.
Naught man could do, have I left undone,
   And you see my harvest, what I reap
This very day, now a year is run.

There 's nobody on the house-tops now, —
   Just a palsied few at the windows set, —
For the best of the sight is, all allow,
   At the Shambles' Gate, — or, better yet,
By the very scaffold's foot, I trow.

I go in the rain, and, more than needs,
   A rope cuts both my wrists behind,
And I think, by the feel, my forehead bleeds,
   For they fling, whoever has a mind,
Stones at me for my year's misdeeds.

Thus I entered Brescia, and thus I go!
  In such triumphs, people have dropped down dead.
"Thou, paid by the World, — what dost thou owe
  Me?" God might have questioned: but now instead
'T is God shall requite! I am safer so.

A GRAMMARIAN'S FUNERAL.

[*Time.* — Shortly after the revival of learning in Europe.]

LET us begin, and carry up this corpse,
　　Singing together.
Leave we the common crofts, the vulgar thorpes,
　　Each in its tether
Sleeping safe on the bosom of the plain,
　　Cared-for till cock-crow.
Look out if yonder 's not the day again
　　Rimming the rock-row !
That 's the appropriate country, — there, man's thought,
　　Rarer, intenser,
Self-gathered for an outbreak, as it ought,
　　Chafes in the censer !
Leave we the unlettered plain its herd and crop :
　　Seek we sepulture
On a tall mountain, citied to the top,
　　Crowded with culture !
All the peaks soar, but one the rest excels ;
　　Clouds overcome it ;
No, yonder sparkle is the citadel's
　　Circling its summit !
Thither our path lies, — wind we up the heights, —
　　Wait ye the warning ?
Our low life was the level's and the night's ;
　　He 's for the morning !
Step to a tune, square chests, erect the head,
　　'Ware the beholders !
This is our master, famous, calm, and dead,
　　Borne on our shoulders.

Sleep, crop and herd !　Sleep, darkling thorpe and croft,
　　Safe from the weather !
He, whom we convoy to his grave aloft,
　　Singing together,

He was a man born with thy face and throat,
    Lyric Apollo!
Long he lived nameless: how should spring take note
    Winter would follow?
Till lo, the little touch, and youth was gone!
    Cramped and diminished,
Moaned he, "New measures, other feet anon!
    My dance is finished?"
No, that's the world's way! (keep the mountain-side,
    Make for the city.)
He knew the signal, and stepped on with pride
    Over men's pity;
Left play for work, and grappled with the world
    Bent on escaping:
"What's in the scroll," quoth he, "thou keepest furled?
    Show me their shaping,
Theirs, who most studied man, the bard and sage, —
    Give!" — So he gowned him,
Straight got by heart that book to its last page:
    Learned, we found him!
Yea, but we found him bald, too, — eyes like lead,
    Accents uncertain:
"Time to taste life," another would have said,
    "Up with the curtain!"
This man said rather, "Actual life comes next?
    Patience a moment!
Grant I have mastered learning's crabbed text,
    Still, there's the comment.
Let me know all. Prate not of most or least,
    Painful or easy:
Even to the crumbs I'd fain eat up the feast,
    Ay, nor feel queasy!"
O, such a life as he resolved to live,
    When he had learned it,
When he had gathered all books had to give;
    Sooner, he spurned it!
Image the whole, then execute the parts, —
    Fancy the fabric
Quite, ere you build, ere steel strike fire from quartz,
    Ere mortar dab brick!

(Here's the town-gate reached : there's the market-place
    Gaping before us.)
Yea, this in him was the peculiar grace
    (Hearten our chorus)
Still before living he'd learn how to live, —
    No end to learning.
Earn the means first, — God surely will contrive
    Use for our earning.
Others mistrust and say, — " But time escapes, —
    Live now or never ! "
He said, " What's Time ? leave Now for dogs and apes !
    Man has Forever."
Back to his book then : deeper drooped his head ;
    Calculus racked him :
Leaden before, his eyes grew dross of lead ;
    Tussis attacked him,
" Now, Master, take a little rest ! " — not he !
    (Caution redoubled !
Step two a-breast, the way winds narrowly.)
    Not a whit troubled,
Back to his studies, fresher than at first,
    Fierce as a dragon
He (soul-hydroptic with a sacred thirst)
    Sucked at the flagon.
O, if we draw a circle premature,
    Heedless of far gain,
Greedy for quick returns of profit, sure,
    Bad is our bargain !
Was it not great ? did he not throw on God,
    (He loves the burthen) —
God's task to make the heavenly period
    Perfect the earthen ?
Did not he magnify the mind, show clear
    Just what it all meant ?
He would not discount life, as fools do here,
    Paid by instalment !
He ventured neck or nothing, — heaven's success
    Found, or earth's failure :
" Wilt thou trust death or not ? " he answered, " Yes.
    Hence with life's pale lure ! "

That low man seeks a little thing to do,
　　Sees it and does it:
This high man, with a great thing to pursue,
　　Dies ere he knows it.
That low man goes on adding one to one,
　　His hundred's soon hit:
This high man, aiming at a million,
　　Misses an unit.
That, has the world here, — should he need the next,
　　Let the world mind him!
This, throws himself on God, and unperplext
　　Seeking shall find Him.
So, with the throttling hands of Death at strife,
　　Ground he at grammar;
Still, through the rattle, parts of speech were rife.
　　While he could stammer
He settled *Hoti's* business, — let it be! —
　　Properly based *Oun*, —
Gave us the doctrine of the enclitic *De*,
　　Dead from the waist down.
Well, here's the platform, here's the proper place.
　　Hail to your purlieus
All ye highfliers of the feathered race,
　　Swallows and curlews!
Here's the top-peak! the multitude below
　　Live, for they can there.
This man decided not to Live but Know, —
　　Bury this man there?
Here, — here's his place, where meteors shoot, clouds form,
　　Lightnings are loosened,
Stars come and go! let joy break with the storm, —
　　Peace let the dew send!
Lofty designs must close in like effects:
　　Loftily lying,
Leave him, — still loftier than the world suspects,
　　Living and dying.

THE CONFESSIONAL.

[SPAIN.]

I T is a lie, — their Priests, their Pope,
  Their Saints, their . . . all they fear or hope
Are lies, and lies, — there! through my door
And ceiling, there!ˌand walls and floor,
There, lies, they lie, shall still be hurled,
Till spite of them I reach the world!

You think Priests just and holy men!
Before they put me in this den,
I was a human creature too,
With flesh and blood like one of you,
A girl that laughed in beauty's pride
Like lilies in your world outside.

I had a lover, — shame avaunt!
This poor wrenched body, grim and gaunt,
Was kissed all over till it burned,
By lips the truest, love e'er turned
Ilis heart's own tint: one night they kissed
My soul out in a burning mist.

So, next day when the accustomed train
Of things grew round my sense again,
" That is a sin," I said, — and slow
With downcast eyes to church I go,
And pass to the confession-chair,
And tell the old mild father there.

But when I falter Beltran's name,
" Ha ? " quoth the father; " much I blame
The sin ; yet wherefore idly grieve ?
Despair not, — strenuously retrieve !
Nay, I will turn this love of thine
To lawful love, almost divine.

" For he is young, and led astray,
This Beltran, and he schemes, men say,
To change the laws of church and state ;
So, thine shall be an angel's fate,
Who, ere the thunder breaks, should roll
Its cloud away and save his soul.

" For, when he lies upon thy breast,
Thou mayst demand and be possessed
Of all his plans, and next day steal
To me, and all those plans reveal,

That I and every priest, to purge
His soul, may fast and use the scourge."

That father's beard was long and white,
With love and truth his brow seemed bright;
I went back, all on fire with joy,
And, that same evening, bade the boy,
Tell me, as lovers should, heart-free,
Something to prove his love of me.

He told me what he would not tell
For hope of Heaven or fear of Hell;
And I lay listening in such pride,
And, soon as he had left my side,
Tripped to the church by morning-light
To save his soul in his despite.

I told the father all his schemes,
Who were his comrades, what their dreams,
"And now make haste," I said, "to pray
The one spot from his soul away:
To-night he comes, but not the same
Will look!" At night he never came.

Nor next night: on the after-morn,
I went forth with a strength new-born:
The church was empty; something drew
My steps into the street; I knew
It led me to the market-place, —
Where, lo! — on high — the father's face!

That horrible black scaffold drest, —
The stapled block . . . God sink the rest!
That head strapped back, that blinding vest,
Those knotted hands and naked breast, —
Till near one busy hangman pressed, —
And — on the neck these arms caressed. . . .

No part in aught they hope or fear!
No Heaven with them, no Hell, — and here,

No Earth, not so much space as pens
My body in their worst of dens
But shall bear God and Man my cry, —
Lies, — lies, again, — and still, they lie!

ONE WAY OF LOVE.

ALL June I bound the rose in sheaves.
　　Now, rose by rose, I strip the leaves,
And strew them where Pauline may pass.
She will not turn aside? Alas!
Let them lie. Suppose they die?
The chance was they might take her eye.

How many a month I strove to suit
These stubborn fingers to the lute!
To-day I venture all I know.
She will not hear my music? So!
Break the string, fold music's wing.
Suppose Pauline had bade me sing!

My whole life long I learned to love.
This hour my utmost art I prove
And speak my passion. — Heaven or hell?
She will not give me heaven? 'T is well!
Lose who may, I still can say,
Those who win heaven, blest are they.

ANOTHER WAY OF LOVE.

JUNE was not over,
   Though past the full,
And the best of her roses
   Had yet to blow,
   When a man I know
(But shall not discover,
   Since ears are dull,
   And time discloses)
Turned him and said, with a man's true air,
Half sighing a smile in a yawn, as 't were, —
" If I tire of your June, will she greatly care ? "

   Well, Dear, in-doors with you !
   True, serene deadness
Tries a man's temper.
   What 's in the blossom
   June wears on her bosom ?
Can it clear scores with you ?
   Sweetness and redness,
   Eadem semper !
Go, let me care for it greatly or slightly !
If June mends her bowers now, your hand left unsightly
By plucking their roses, — my June will do rightly.

   And after, for pastime,
   If June be refulgent
With flowers in completeness,
   All petals, no prickles,
   Delicious as trickles
Of wine poured at mass-time, —
   And choose One indulgent
   To redness and sweetness :
Or if, with experience of man and of spider,
She use my June-lightning, the strong insect-ridder,
To stop the fresh spinning, — why, June will consider.

7

MISCONCEPTIONS.

THIS is a spray the Bird clung to,
    Making it blossom with pleasure,
Ere the high tree-top she sprung to,
    Fit for her nest and her treasure.
    O, what a hope beyond measure
Was the poor spray's, which the flying feet hung to, —
    So to be singled out, built in, and sung to!

This is a heart the Queen leant on,
    Thrilled in a minute erratic,
Ere the true bosom she bent on,
    Meet for love's regal dalmatic.
    O, what a fancy ecstatic
Was the poor heart's, ere the wanderer went on, —
    Love to be saved for it, proffered to, spent on!

ONE WORD MORE.

TO E. B. B.

THERE they are, my fifty men and women
    Naming me the fifty poems finished!
Take them, Love, the book and me together.
Where the heart lies, let the brain lie also.

Rafael made a century of sonnets,
Made and wrote them in a certain volume
Dinted with the silver-pointed pencil
Else he only used to draw Madonnas:

These, the world might view, — but One, the volume.
Who that one, you ask?   Your heart instructs you.
Did she live and love it all her lifetime?
Did she drop, his lady of the sonnets,
Die, and let it drop beside her pillow
Where it lay in place of Rafael's glory,
Rafael's cheek so duteous and so loving, —
Cheek, the world was wont to hail a painter's,
Rafael's cheek, her love had turned a poet's?

You and I would rather read that volume,
(Taken to his beating bosom by it,)
Lean and list the bosom-beats of Rafael,
Would we not? than wonder at Madonnas, —
Her, San Sisto names, and Her, Foligno,
Her, that visits Florence in a vision,
Her, that 's left with lilies in the Louvre, —
Seen by us and all the world in circle.

You and I will never read that volume.
Guido Reni, like his own eye's apple
Guarded long the treasure-book and loved it.
Guido Reni dying, all Bologna
Cried, and the world with it, "Ours — the treasure!"
Suddenly, as rare things will, it vanished.

Dante once prepared to paint an angel:
Whom to please?   You whisper "Beatrice."
While he mused and traced it and retraced it,
(Peradventure with a pen corroded
Still by drops of that hot ink he dipped for,
When, his left-hand i' the hair o' the wicked,
Back he held the brow and pricked its stigma,
Bit into the live man's flesh for parchment,
Loosed him, laughed to see the writing rankle,
Let the wretch go festering through Florence,) —
Dante, who loved well because he hated,
Hated wickedness that hinders loving,
Dante standing, studying his angel, —

In there broke the folk of his Inferno.
Says he, — " Certain people of importance "
(Such he gave his daily, dreadful line to)
Entered and would seize, forsooth, the poet.
Says the poet, — " Then I stopped my painting."

You and I would rather see that angel,
Painted by the tenderness of Dante,
Would we not ? — than read a fresh Inferno.

You and I will never see that picture.
While he mused on love and Beatrice,
While he softened o'er his outlined angel,
In they broke, those " people of importance " :
We and Bice bear the loss forever.

What of Rafael's sonnets, Dante's picture ?

This : no artist lives and loves that longs not
Once, and only once, and for One only,
(Ah, the prize !) to find his love a language
Fit and fair and simple and sufficient, —
Using nature that 's an art to others,
Not, this one time, art that 's turned his nature.
Ay, of all the artists living, loving,
None but would forego his proper dowry, —
Does he paint ? he fain would write a poem, —
Does he write ? he fain would paint a picture,
Put to proof art alien to the artist's,
Once, and only once, and for One only,
So to be the man and leave the artist,
Save the man's joy, miss the artist's sorrow.

Wherefore ?   Heaven's gift takes earth's abatement !
He who smites the rock and spreads the water,
Bidding drink and live a crowd beneath him,
Even he, the minute makes immortal,
Proves, perchance, his mortal in the minute,
Desecrates, belike, the deed in doing.

While he smites, how can he but remember,
So he smote before, in such a peril,
When they stood and mocked, — "Shall smiting help us?"
When they drank and sneered, — "A stroke is easy!"
When they wiped their mouths and went their journey,
Throwing him for thanks, — "But drought was pleasant."
Thus old memories mar the actual triumph;
Thus the doing savors of disrelish;
Thus achievement lacks a gracious somewhat;
O'er-importuned brows becloud the mandate,
Carelessness or consciousness, the gesture.
For he bears an ancient wrong about him,
Sees and knows again those phalanxed faces,
Hears, yet one time more, the 'customed prelude, —
"How shouldst thou, of all men, smite, and save us?"
Guesses what is like to prove the sequel, —
"Egypt's flesh-pots, — nay, the drought was better."

O, the crowd must have emphatic warrant!
Theirs, the Sinai-forehead's cloven brilliance,
Right-arm's rod-sweep, tongue's imperial fiat.
Never dares the man put off the prophet.

Did he love one face from out the thousands,
(Where she Jethro's daughter, white and wifely,
Were she but the Æthiopian bond-slave,)
He would envy yon dumb patient camel,
Keeping a reserve of scanty water
Meant to save his own life in the desert;
Ready in the desert to deliver
(Kneeling down to let his breast be opened)
Hoard and life together for his mistress.

I shall never, in the years remaining,
Paint you pictures, no, nor carve you statues,
Make you music that should all-express me;
So it seems: I stand on my attainment.
This of verse alone, one life allows me;
Verse and nothing else have I to give you.

Other heights in other lives, God willing, —
All the gifts from all the heights, your own, Love!

Yet a semblance of resource avails us, —
Shade so finely touched, love's sense must seize it.
Take these lines, look lovingly and nearly,
Lines I write the first time and the last time.
He who works in fresco, steals a hair-brush,
Curbs the liberal hand, subservient proudly,
Cramps his spirit, crowds its all in little,
Makes a strange art of an art familiar,
Fills his lady's missal-marge with flowerets.
He who blows through bronze, may breathe through silver,
Fitly serenade a slumbrous princess.
He who writes, may write for once, as I do.

Love, you saw me gather men and women,
Live or dead or fashioned by my fancy,
Enter each and all, and use their service,
Speak from every mouth, — the speech, a poem.
Hardly shall I tell my joys and sorrows,
Hopes and fears, belief and disbelieving:
I am mine and yours, — the rest be all men's,
Karshook, Cleon, Norbert, and the fifty.
Let me speak this once in my true person,
Not as Lippo, Roland, or Andrea,
Though the fruit of speech be just this sentence, —
Pray you, look on these my men and women,
Take and keep my fifty poems finished;
Where my heart lies, let my brain lie also!
Poor the speech; be how I speak, for all things.

Not but that you know me! Lo! the moon's self!
Here in London, yonder late in Florence,
Still we find her face, the thrice-transfigured.
Curving on a sky imbrued with color,
Drifted over Fiesole by twilight,
Came she, our new crescent of a hair's-breadth.
Full she flared it, lamping Samminiato,

Rounder 'twixt the cypresses and rounder,
Perfect till the nightingales applauded.
Now, a piece of her old self, impoverished,
Hard to greet, she traverses the house-roofs,
Hurries with unhandsome thrift of silver,
Goes dispiritedly, — glad to finish.

What, there's nothing in the moon note-worthy?
Nay, — for if that moon could love a mortal,
Use, to charm him (so to fit a fancy)
All her magic ('t is the old sweet mythos)
She would turn a new side to her mortal,
Side unseen of herdsman, huntsman, steersman, —
Blank to Zoroaster on his terrace,
Blind to Galileo on his turret,
Dumb to Homer, dumb to Keats, — him, even!
Think, the wonder of the moonstruck mortal, —
When she turns round, comes again in heaven,
Opens out anew for worse or better?
Proves she like some portent of an iceberg
Swimming full upon the ship it founders,
Hungry with huge teeth of splintered crystals?
Proves she as the paved-work of a sapphire
Seen by Moses when he climbed the mountain?
Moses, Aaron, Nadab and Abihu
Climbed and saw the very God, the Highest,
Stand upon the paved-work of a sapphire.
Like the bodied heaven in his clearness
Shone the stone, the sapphire of that paved-work,
When they ate and drank and saw God also!

What were seen? None knows, none ever shall know.
Only this is sure, — the sight were other,
Not the moon's same side, born late in Florence,
Dying now impoverished here in London.
God be thanked, the meanest of his creatures
Boasts two soul-sides, one to face the world with,
One to show a woman when he loves her.

This I say of me, but think of you, Love!
This to you, — yourself my moon of poets!
Ah, but that's the world's side, — there's the wonder, —
Thus they see you, praise you, think they know you.
There, in turn I stand with them and praise you,
Out of my own self, I dare to phrase it.
But the best is when I glide from out them,
Cross a step or two of dubious twilight,
Come out on the other side, the novel
Silent silver lights and darks undreamed of,
Where I hush and bless myself with silence.

O, their Rafael of the dear Madonnas,
O, their Dante of the dread Inferno,
Wrote one song — and in my brain I sing it,
Drew one angel — borne, see, on my bosom!

MEETING AT NIGHT.

THE gray sea and the long black land;
  And the yellow half-moon large and low;
And the startled little waves that leap
In fiery ringlets from their sleep,
As I gain the cove with pushing prow,
And quench its speed in the slushy sand.

Then a mile of warm sea-scented beach;
Three fields to cross till a farm appears;
A tap at the pane, the quick sharp scratch
And blue spurt of a lighted match,
And a voice less loud, through its joys and fears,
Than the two hearts beating each to each!

PARTING AT MORNING.

ROUND the cape of a sudden came the sea,
    And the sun looked over the mountain's rim, —
And straight was a path of gold for him,
And the need of a world of men for me.

PROSPICE.

FEAR death? — to feel the fog in my throat,
    The mist in my face,
When the snows begin, and the blasts denote
    I am nearing the place,
The power of the night, the press of the storm,
    The post of the foe;
Where he stands, the Arch Fear in a visible form,
    Yet the strong man must go:
For the journey is done and the summit attained,
    And the barriers fall,
Though a battle 's to fight ere the guerdon be gained,
    The reward of it all.
I was ever a fighter, so, — one fight more,
    The best and the last!
I would hate that death bandaged my eyes, and forbore,
    And bade me creep past.
No! let me taste the whole of it, fare like my peers
    The heroes of old,
Bear the brunt, in a minute pay glad life's arrears
    Of pain, darkness, and cold.
For sudden the worst turns the best to the brave,
    The black minute 's at end,

And the elements' rage, the fiend-voices that rave,
    Shall dwindle, shall blend,
Shall change, shall become first a peace, then a joy,
    Then a light, then thy breast,
O thou soul of my soul! I shall clasp thee again,
    And with God be the rest!

MAY AND DEATH.

I WISH that when you died last May,
    Charles, there had died along with you
Three parts of spring's delightful things;
    Ay, and, for me, the fourth part too.

A foolish thought, and worse, perhaps!
    There must be many a pair of friends
Who, arm in arm, deserve the warm
    Moon-births and the long evening-ends.

So, for their sakes, be May still May!
    Let their new time, as mine of old,
Do all it did for me: I bid
    Sweet sights and sounds throng manifold.

Only, one little sight, one plant,
    Woods have in May, that starts up green
Save a sole streak which, so to speak,
    Is spring's blood, spilt its leaves between, —

That, they might spare; a certain wood
    Might miss the plant; their loss were small:
But I, — whene'er the leaf grows there,
    Its drop comes from my heart, that's all.

IN THE DOORWAY.

THE swallow has set her six young on the rail,
      And looks seaward :
The water 's in stripes like a snake, olive-pale
      To the leeward, —
On the weather-side, black, spotted white with the wind :
" Good fortune departs, and disaster 's behind," —
Hark, the wind with its wants and its infinite wail!

Our fig-tree, that leaned for the saltness, has furled
      Her five fingers,
Each leaf like a hand opened wide to the world
      Where there lingers
No glint of the gold, Summer sent for her sake :
How the vines writhe in rows, each impaled on its stake !
My heart shrivels up, and my spirit shrinks curled.

Yet here are we two ; we have love, house enough,
      With the field there,
This house of four rooms, that field red and rough,
      Though it yield there,
For the rabbit that robs, scarce a blade or a bent ;
If a magpie alight now, it seems an event ;
And they both will be gone at November's rebuff.

But why must cold spread ? but wherefore bring change
      To the spirit,
God meant should mate His with an infinite range,
      And inherit
His power to put life in the darkness and cold ?
O, live and love worthily, bear and be bold !
Whom Summer made friends of, let Winter estrange !

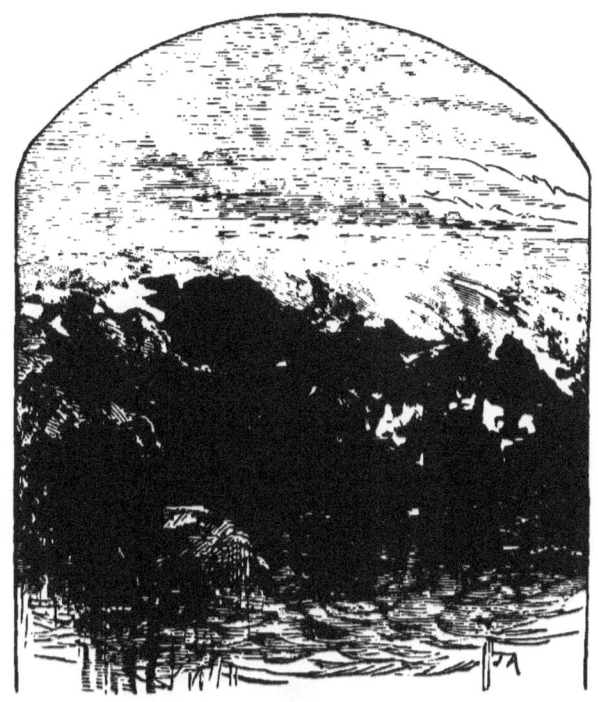

AMONG THE ROCKS.

O GOOD, gigantic smile o' the brown old earth,
    This autumn morning! How he sets his bones
To bask i' the sun, and thrusts out knees and feet
For the ripple to run over in its mirth;
    Listening the while, where on the heap of stones
The white breast of the sea-lark twitters sweet.

That is the doctrine, simple, ancient, true;
    Such is life's trial, as old earth smiles and knows.
If you loved only what were worth your love,
Love were clear gain, and wholly well for you:
    Make the low nature better by your throes!
Give earth yourself, go up for gain above!

Cambridge: Printed by Welch, Bigelow, & Co.